The Three Little Pigs

Illustrated by Pam Storey
Story re-told by Grace De La Touche

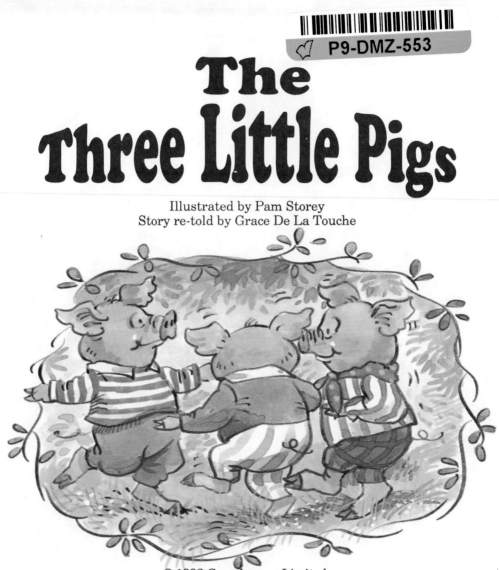

© 1992 Grandreams Limited.

This edition published in 1994.

Published by
Grandreams Limited
Jadwin House, 205/211 Kentish Town Road, London, NW5 2JU.

Printed in Italy.

GS5-8

A long time ago and far away there lived
a Mother Pig and her three sons. The three
Little Pigs were growing bigger and bigger
every day.

"It really is time you moved out and made
homes for yourselves," said Mother Pig one day.
"This place isn't big enough for all of us."

The very next day the three Little Pigs
moved out, taking their belongings with them.

"Watch out for the Big Bad Wolf," said Mother Pig as they left.

They set off down the road and came to a crossroads. Each Little Pig went in a different direction.

The youngest one headed for the fields.

"I want to have fun," he said. "My house will be very quick to build." He cut lots of hay and straw and made himself a straw house with a thatched roof.

The house was soon finished and he moved in at the end of the day. His house may have been quick but it wasn't very strong.

Someone had
been watching him
while he had been
building it. The Big
Bad Wolf in the forest
nearby was very fond
of Little Pigs. He
liked eating them!

The youngest
Little Pig had settled
down for the evening
when there was a knock at his door.

"Who's there?" asked the Little Pig. No-
one knew where he lived yet.

"Let me in, Little Pig, let me in," said a deep voice. "Or by the hair on my chinny chin chin, I'll blow your house down."

"It's the Big Bad Wolf," cried the Little Pig. "Just like Mother Pig said."

"Open the door, Little Pig," said the Big Bad Wolf again.

"No!" shouted the Little Pig. "I won't let you in!"

"Then," said the Big Bad Wolf. "I'll huff and I'll puff and I'll blow your house down!"

The Big Bad Wolf huffed and he puffed, and he blew the straw house down. The Little Pig ran and ran.

The second Little Pig had headed for the woods.

"I want to spend time looking in the woods, not building my house," he said. "My house will be very quick to build." He gathered

lots of twigs and sticks and made himself a house of sticks.

His house was very quick to build and he moved in at the end of the day. His house may have been quick, but it was not very strong.

Someone had been watching him while he was building it. The Big Bad Wolf in the forest liked eating Little Pigs and he had missed the first Little Pig.

The second Little Pig had settled down for the evening when there was a knock at his door. "Who's there?" asked the Little Pig. No-one knew where he lived yet.

"Let me in, Little Pig, let me in," said the Wolf. "Or by the hair on my chinny chin chin, I'll blow your house down."

"It's the Big Bad Wolf," cried the Little Pig. "Just like Mother Pig said."

"Open the door, Little Pig," said the Big Bad Wolf again.

"No!" shouted the Little Pig. "I won't let you in!"

"Then," said the Big Bad Wolf. "I'll huff and I'll puff and I'll blow your house down!"

The Big Bad Wolf huffed and he puffed, and he blew the stick house down. The Little Pig ran and ran.

The second Little Pig met the first Little
Pig running along the road to the crossroads
where they had separated such a short while
before. They set off down the road that their
older brother had taken.

The third Little Pig had decided to make
a good, strong house for himself.

"I don't want to be eaten by the Big Bad
Wolf," he said. He headed for the town and

bought lots of bricks and cement and then, some way out of town, he built his new home.

His house was made of bricks and would not fall down in a puff of wind. He had windows and a chimney, and a rocking chair in front of the fire.

The Little Pig's house was not built in a day, so he spent the night in a very comfortable hotel.

When his
house was ready, he
moved in. He had
just settled down to
an evening in front
of the fire when
there was a knock
at the door.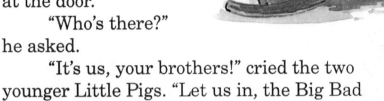

"Who's there?"
he asked.

"It's us, your brothers!" cried the two
younger Little Pigs. "Let us in, the Big Bad
Wolf is after us."

The third Little Pig jumped up to let
them in. He couldn't let the horrible wolf catch
his young brothers.

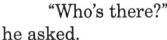

The two Little Pigs told their older
brother what had happened.

"That's what comes from not building
proper houses," he told them. "We'll be safe
here."

At that moment there was a knock on the
door.

The two Little Pigs shook and shivered.

The third Little Pig stood by the door and said, "Who's there?"

"Let me in, Little Pig, let me in," said the Big Bad Wolf. "Or by the hair on my chinny chin chin, I'll blow your house down."

"No!" shouted the Little Pig. "I won't let you in."

The Big Bad Wolf huffed and he puffed, then he puffed and he huffed. The little brick house did not move.

The Big Bad Wolf huffed and puffed until

he was blue in the face, but he could not blow the Little Pig's house down.

He went away to think about things, but he was back the next morning.

"Little Pig," he called to the Little Pig in the house. "The market is coming to town tomorrow. Why don't I meet you on the road to town and we can go to market together."

"That would be very nice," said the Little Pig. "I'll meet you at eight o'clock by the milestone."

The next morning the Big Bad Wolf was
at the milestone at quarter to eight. He was
determined to catch the Little Pig.

But the Little Pig was much too clever to
be caught. He had been to the market and back
again by half past seven. The Big Bad Wolf had
been waiting for nothing and he was very
angry.

He realised that the Little Pig had been too clever for him, and went back to the Little Pig's house.

"Little Pig," he called out. "The apples in the orchard are just turning ripe! Why don't we pick some together. You will be far too short to reach the branches, maybe I can help."

"That's very kind of you," said the Little Pig. "I'll meet you by the orchard gate at two in the afternoon, just after lunch."

"I'll be there," said the Big Bad Wolf. And he was. He was there at twelve o'clock - before lunch!

But the Little Pig had been clever again, and had gone to the orchard at ten o'clock!

But guess who was waiting at the orchard gate when he left at twelve o'clock. The Big Bad Wolf was too busy looking at the Little Pig's house to see the Little Pig coming from behind him, and the next moment he was bowled over as the Little Pig went rolling by in a barrel!

The Little Pig jumped out and ran indoors, just as the Big Bad Wolf reached the garden gate.

"I'll get you," cried the Big Bad Wolf, and he saw the three Little Pigs looking out of the window and laughing at him. He disappeared into the forest.

The three Little Pigs sat and laughed.

"That must be the last that we'll see of him," said the first Little Pig. "He knows he'll never catch us."

"Don't be so sure," said the third Little Pig. "Here he comes now!"

"What is he carrying?" asked the second Little Pig.

"It's a ladder!" said the third Little Pig. "And I think I know what he plans to do with it."

The two younger Little Pigs watched the Big Bad Wolf as he came nearer to the house. The older Little Pig was bustling round by the fireplace.

"I think this will soon put a stop to his games," said the third Little Pig.

He had quickly made a fire and it was beginning to burn well. He moved a huge pot onto the fire and filled it with water.

He rubbed his hands together.

"What are we going to do?" cried the two Little Pigs.

"Listen, you can hear him. He's on the roof. What shall we do?"

"Nothing," said their brother. "I've done it. Wait and see what happens. After this we won't be bothered by the Big Bad Wolf again."

There was a sudden scrambling inside the chimney as the Big Bad Wolf started to climb down.

"Aieee!" yelled the Big Bad Wolf, as he suddenly realised that the chimney was warm and getting even warmer. He scrabbled and scrambled, trying to get back up the chimney, but he couldn't!

"Aagh!" yelled the Big Bad Wolf as he came tumbling down the chimney.

SPLASH! The wolf landed in the huge pot of simmering water that the third Little Pig had put on the flames.